DISNEY'S

THE LITTLE MERMAID

THE SAME OLD SONG

by Marilyn Kaye

illustrations by Fred Marvin

DISNEY PRESS

NEW YORK

For Lauren and Katy

Produced by arrangement with Chardiet Unlimited, Inc.

Library of Congress Catalog Card Number: 92-53936

ISBN: 1-56282-249-7

FIRST EDITION

1 3 5 7 9 10 8 6 4 2

Under the sea, the sparkling blue water was warm and crystal clear. Ariel, the youngest of King Triton's seven daughters, swam in a circle around two of her older sisters. Carelessly pushing her long red hair from her face, she smiled, and her big blue eyes twinkled.

"I love weekends!" she announced. "No school, no homework, and no music lessons. We're free to do anything we want!"

"And I want to have some fun," Alana declared, tugging at her black pigtails.

"Me, too," Andrina agreed.

"What shall we do today?" Ariel asked.

"Let's ride sea horses," Andrina suggested. The most athletic of the sisters, Andrina always wanted to do something active.

"The snails are having a relay race today," Alana reported. "We can watch that."

"Or we could explore some caves," Andrina offered. "What do you think, Ariel?"

Ariel couldn't decide. There were so many good times to be had on a beautiful day like this. How could she choose?

"I know," she cried. "Let's do everything!"

"Here come Arista and Aquata," Andrina said as she waved to her other sisters. "Come on!" she called. "We're going to ride sea horses and watch the snails race and explore caves."

"Oh no you're not," Arista replied knowingly. "You're not doing any of those things."

Andrina shot a look at her sister. She could tell by the expression on Arista's face that something was up—something big. "What's going on?" she asked her.

"Sebastian wants to see us," Aquata answered before Arista could get the chance. *"Now."*

Ariel was confused. "Sebastian?" she asked. "Why would Sebastian want to see us today? Our next music lesson isn't until Tuesday."

"We don't know," Arista answered. "He just said he wants all of us to meet him at the Great Concert Hall right away."

Alana, who hardly ever worried about anything, asked, "Are we in trouble?"

"What are you so nervous about?" Ariel asked. "You know Sebastian. He fusses sometimes, but he never gets really angry."

"Hurry up," Aquata said. "We have to find Adella and Attina. I think they're back at the palace."

When the mermaids reached the palace, they swam up to Attina's bedroom. There they found their sister, curled up with a book, twisting a lock of her light brown hair. Attina spent every Saturday doing the same thing. She was definitely the bookworm of the family.

"We have to meet Sebastian at the concert hall," Arista reported.

"Can't you see I'm reading?" Attina looked up, ready to protest, but then she noticed the looks on her sisters' faces. Without another word, she placed a piece of seaweed in the

3

book to mark her place and followed the others.

Adella was in her usual place, too: admiring herself in front of her bedroom mirror, weaving a string of beads through her jet black hair. When she heard the news, she frowned. "I was going to try a new hairstyle today."

"Whatever Sebastian wants is more important than your hair," Aquata said sternly.

Adella pouted, put down her hairbrush, and followed her sisters out the door.

Sebastian, the royal court composer, was waiting for the mermaids in the concert hall, scuttling back and forth on the concert stage, muttering to himself with excitement. Ariel breathed a sigh of relief when she saw him. He didn't look angry or upset at all.

Sebastian rubbed his claws together and beamed at the mermaids. "Well, my little princesses, it's that time again!"

"Time for what?" Ariel asked.

"For the annual Under the Sea Musical Gala!"

All the mermaids groaned. "Is it that time already?" Attina asked. "Didn't we just have a musical gala?"

Sebastian ignored her. "In just two weeks," he continued, "all the merpeople of the sea will gather here in my . . . er . . . in *our* Great Concert Hall for a grand concert presented by the daughters of His Majesty, King Triton. And I intend to make sure you give them a good one!" He stood with his chest puffed out with determination and a claw raised above his head for effect.

"Now listen here, Princesses," he went on. "I've just received word from your father that he has invited the Grand Mer-Rajah of the Indian Ocean to be his special guest at the gala. The King has requested a particularly extraordinary performance in honor of his distinguished guest, so we haven't a single minute to waste!" He began passing around sheet music to the mermaids, ignoring their pouty expressions.

"Now," he said, clearing his throat, "we'll begin today's rehearsal right now, and we'll rehearse all day tomorrow and every single day after your lessons. Come to think of it, maybe we'll rehearse in the morning, before your lessons, as well."

"But Sebastian . . . ," they protested.

"Yes, it's a marvelous idea," he said, not letting them finish. "Bright and early before school. Ah, but we're wasting precious rehearsal time right now just talking about it! Let's start right away. Take a look at the sheet music I've handed out. I have composed some wonderful songs for you this year, and I must admit," he chuckled with delight, "they are simply enchanting! Hmmm . . . I don't seem to have an extra copy for myself. Wait right here, my dears, I think I may have another copy back at my office."

As soon as Sebastian was out of earshot, Andrina groaned. "Another musical gala. Good-bye, weekends!"

"Rehearse *before* school?" Adella asked. Her face was glum.

Arista sighed. "Day after day."

Alana nodded. "Hour after hour."

Attina cast a sad glance at the book she was holding. "I won't have any time to read."

"I like singing in the gala," Ariel offered.

"Of course *you* do," Adella snapped at her sister. "Sebastian always gives you the good songs to sing."

"Everyone knows that's because Ariel has

the prettiest voice," Alana noted.

Adella sniffed. "But that means *she* always gets to be the star."

"It's not the *singing* I mind," Arista complained. "It's the practicing."

"And the way Sebastian nags us," Alana added. "He's so fussy."

Andrina agreed. "And the way he makes us sing every line, over and over and over again."

"Well, there's nothing we can do about it," Aquata said. "We have to perform at the gala. Father would have a fit if we didn't." They all agreed.

"Wait!" Attina said suddenly. "Maybe there *is* something we can do about it."

The other mermaids looked at her in surprise. "What?" Ariel asked.

"I know we have to perform in the gala every year," Attina said. "But why does it always have to be a concert?"

"What else can we do?" Aquata asked.

"We could put on a play instead," Attina suggested.

"Sebastian writes music," Ariel pointed out. "He doesn't write plays."

Attina blushed. "I . . . um . . . I wrote a play."

Ariel clapped her hands. "You did? Attina! That's wonderful!"

"A play!" Adella exclaimed. "What a super idea!"

The mermaids gathered around Attina. "What is your play about?" Andrina asked her.

"Well . . . it's about a family of mermaids," Attina told them.

"It would be fun to do a play instead of a concert," Alana said. "And how much work could it be if we're just playing mermaids?"

Adella nodded. "I *do* have the looks to be an actress."

Ariel rolled her eyes. Adella was so vain!

"Let's do it!" Arista declared.

"It's an interesting idea," Aquata said slowly. "But we'll have to run it by Sebastian first."

The mermaids looked at each other. Telling Sebastian was going to be the hard part. He had his heart set on a concert. Who would be brave enough to break the news to him? All eyes turned toward Ariel.

Sebastian hurried back into the hall, clutching a pile of sheet music in his claws. "Come closer, Princesses. I want you to hear all the new songs I've composed. I must say, in all modesty, they are the best I have ever written."

The mermaids looked at Ariel. Ariel bit her lip and swallowed nervously. Arista nudged her forward.

"Sebastian," Ariel began, her voice cracking. "Uh, there's something we want to ask you. You see, um, Attina has written a play."

"That's nice," Sebastian murmured. He was busy studying the sheet music and humming to himself. "Ah yes, this is an enchanting melody, if I do say so myself."

"Sebastian," Ariel said, raising her voice, "did you hear what I just said?"

Sebastian stopped humming. He looked at Ariel.

Ariel took a deep breath and spoke quickly. "We would like to present Attina's play for the annual gala. Instead of giving a concert."

Sebastian's eyes widened.

"What? What silliness is this?" he cried, swimming over to the mermaids. "My dear princesses, you cannot perform a play instead of a concert!"

"Why not?" Andrina challenged.

"Yes, why not?" Alana echoed.

"Why not?" Sebastian screeched. "Why not?"

His face became redder than ever. "I'll tell you why not! Because this is the Under the Sea *Musical* Gala! *Musical!* That means a concert! It has always been a concert, and it will always be a concert. It is a tradition!"

"But Sebastian," Ariel argued. "You said that Father wanted something extraordinary. A play would be more unusual than a concert."

"I'll hear no more of this nonsense," Sebastian declared. He shuffled his sheet music and dismissed their notion with a wave of his claw. "Every year, we give a concert. Your father, His Great and Noble Majesty, King Triton, expects to hear a concert. All the merpeople of the kingdom expect to hear a concert. And you, my dear princesses . . . "

The mermaids finished the sentence for him. " . . . are going to give a concert."

But none of them sounded very happy about it.

Sebastian tapped his conductor's baton on a clamshell to get the mermaids' attention. "Ahem," he said, clearing his throat. "Let us begin immediately!"

Sebastian leaned over the edge of the stage and shouted, "Octavio! Octavio! We are ready for you."

Slowly a giant clamshell orchestra pit began to rise up from below. A large octopus surrounded by musical instruments slithered into position and prepared to play. With two tentacles, he raised a flute to his mouth. He gathered a violin and a bow in another two tentacles. His fifth tentacle wrapped around a cello, while the sixth lifted a long bow. And with his last two tentacles Octavio played the piano.

While Octavio tuned his instruments, Alana whispered to Andrina, "I guess we'll just have to make the best of this."

Andrina nodded. "Maybe Sebastian won't be as strict with us this year as he was last year."

"No talking, please!" Sebastian yelled. "Keep your mouths closed!"

"That will make it kind of hard to sing, won't it?" Andrina replied with a grin. Her sisters couldn't help but laugh.

"And no joking, either!" Sebastian cried even louder, putting an end to their giggling. "Singing is serious business! Now, please look at the first sheet. This is a song about the beauty of the sea in the evening. I want to hear the first two lines. In C minor, please."

Octavio started to play, Sebastian waved his baton, and the mermaids began to sing.

Oh, what a lovely sight,
Our ocean world by night.
The . . .

"No, no, no!" Sebastian exclaimed. "You are saying these words as if they mean nothing! Where is the feeling? Think about the beauty you are describing! Again," Sebastian demanded.

After the fourth time, they finally managed to get through the entire song without stopping, although Sebastian gave orders through it all. "The tempo, the tempo! You are singing too slowly! Where's the expression in your voice?"

Sebastian shook his head wearily. "Well," he sighed, "we will come back to this song a little later. Let us move on to 'When You Wish upon a Fish.' Now, where did I put the music?" He scurried about, searching for the sheet music.

"There's Flounder!" Andrina told Ariel.

Ariel brightened when she saw her best friend swimming toward them. She waved to him happily.

"Hi, Flounder. What are you doing here?" she asked.

"I wanted to hear you sing," he replied.

"Did you see the snail races?" Andrina asked eagerly.

"Yes, and they were so exciting!" Flounder told them. "I have never seen snails move so fast!"

"Who won?" Alana asked.

Flounder didn't have time to answer her. Sebastian had returned from his office, carrying another clawful of music. He frowned when he saw Flounder. "No visitors!" he barked. "No onlookers, no watchers!"

"But he just wants to listen," Ariel said.

"No listeners!"

"But it's Flounder, Sebastian," Ariel protested. "He's our friend."

"No friends, no enemies," Sebastian stated. "We will have no audience for our rehearsals. The Under the Sea Musical Gala must be a surprise for all!"

Disappointed, Flounder swam slowly out of the hall. "What a grouch," Andrina muttered.

"Quiet!" Sebastian bellowed. "Enough goofing around. Here is the music for the next song. This will be a solo for Ariel."

"Why does Ariel always get the solos?"

Adella complained. "*I* want to sing a solo."

"That's okay with me," Ariel said. "Sebastian, can Adella sing this solo instead of me?"

"She may," Sebastian said, raising an eyebrow in Adella's direction. "Of course, this will mean extra practice for her," he added. "Evenings, days, weekends, her lunch and dinner hours. And every Saturday night from now until the gala."

"Forget it," Adella said quickly. "I changed my mind. Let Ariel sing it."

"I thought you might say that," Sebastian muttered knowingly.

Ariel sighed. "We need a break, Sebastian. Isn't it time for lunch?"

"It must be," Andrina said. "I'm starved." The mermaids looked hopefully at Sebastian.

"I have arranged to have our lunch brought here," he told them. "We have no time for breaks."

The sisters looked at each other in despair. There was no escape!

Sebastian ordered the mermaids to sit quietly while Ariel learned her solo. Usually Sebastian was pleased with Ariel's singing, but this time even her sweet, melodic voice didn't satisfy him. She barely got three words out of her mouth before he rapped his baton and stopped her. "Louder!" he cried out. "Keep the rhythm! Enunciate! Articulate!"

Ariel had to sing the song twice more before Sebastian seemed satisfied. Finally, after the third time, Sebastian said, "Thank you, my dear, that will be all."

The sisters exchanged expressions of relief. "Well, it's about time," Adella said. "I don't know how much more of this I can take."

Andrina stretched as she got up from her seat. "I don't know about you girls, but I'm beat!"

"Me, too," Alana said, starting toward the exit.

A thundering voice stopped them in their tracks. "Where do you think you're going?" Sebastian bellowed. "We are not finished here!"

"But Sebastian," Andrina protested, "you said we were finished."

"I said nothing of the sort," Sebastian declared. "I merely expressed my gratitude to Ariel for singing her solo so beautifully. As for the rest of you, it's back to the beginning. And this time—with feeling!"

The mermaids groaned and grudgingly returned to the stage. Adella was furious. "He's gone mad," she whispered to Aquata. "He's treating us like prisoners!"

"Shh," Sebastian ordered. "Line up on the stage, and we'll take it from the top."

"Look," Andrina exclaimed, pointing to the rear of the hall.

Everyone turned to see a small crayfish enter the enormous concert hall. Now this was something! They hardly ever saw crayfish in this part of the sea. They lived in warmer waters.

Crayfish or not, Sebastian wasn't pleased to see this stranger at all. "No visitors!" he yelled from the stage.

"But I have an urgent message," the crayfish said in a scratchy voice. He held a shell in his hand.

Excitedly Adella wriggled out of line. She was always getting messages from mermen who admired her. "Is it for me?" she asked, batting her eyelashes.The crayfish examined the shell. "Are you Sebastian, royal court

18

composer and conductor?" he asked.

"No," Adella mumbled in disappointment.

Sebastian crawled over to the crayfish. "I am the royal composer. Give me the message."

The crayfish turned the shell over to Sebastian, whipped around, and made his way to the door. Sebastian put the shell down and went back to the mermaids.

"Aren't you going to read it?" Arista asked.

"Later," Sebastian said. "We have too much work to do now."

"But it might be important," Ariel said.

"Yes, it could be from Father," Andrina added, knowing very well that the message couldn't possibly be from King Triton. The mermaids' father didn't have any crayfish messengers. But Andrina also knew that Sebastian would interrupt anything for the King.

Sebastian perked up. "I suppose that's possible," he said, picking up the shell. Peering inside to read the message, his deep crimson complexion lightened to pink. "Oh my!" he exclaimed.

The mermaids hurried over to him. "What's wrong?" Aquata asked anxiously.

"Is it bad news?" Arista asked.

When Sebastian spoke, his voice was faint. "No, no, nothing is wrong, it is not bad news. In fact, it is . . . something quite remarkable." His eyes gleamed, and the color returned to his face. "I have been invited to be a guest conductor at the Dixieland Waters Jazz Festival."

"How wonderful!" Ariel exclaimed.

"That's a great honor," Aquata added.

Arista clapped her hands together. "We're so proud of you, Sebastian! Why, you will become famous!"

"Yes, yes, it is wonderful," Sebastian said softly. "Or should I say, it *would have been* wonderful." The gleam was gone from his eyes as he said, "Unfortunately, I cannot go."

The mermaids were surprised. "Why can't you go, Sebastian?" Ariel asked.

Sebastian showed them the message. "Dear princesses, look at the date of the festival. If I were to accept this invitation, I would have to leave today. I cannot abandon you now! We have to practice for the gala."

"We could skip a few rehearsals," Andrina said eagerly. "It's okay with us. Really."

Alana swished her tail through the water and nudged Andrina lightly. "We don't have to miss any rehearsals," she said. "We can practice on our own."

"That's right, Sebastian," Aquata added. "And haven't you always said how much you dreamed of conducting a real jazz band someday? This is your big chance!"

"That is true," Sebastian said sadly. "But my dear princesses come first."

"We don't mind being second," Andrina said.

Sebastian was torn. He looked at the message again. "No, no, it is impossible for me to go." He shook his head. "It's out of the question. Why, the jazz festival lasts for two weeks. If I were to go, I wouldn't even make it back here in time for the gala!"

"That's truly a shame," Arista said. "I'm sure the merpeople of the Dixieland Waters will be terribly disappointed."

"Oh, yes," Attina agreed. "They must know that you are the greatest conductor and composer of all the seas."

"Their festival cannot possibly be a success without you," Adella stated firmly.

Just then the doors to the concert hall opened. Stately sea horse messengers entered.

One cried out, "All hail His Majesty, the noble Triton, King of the Sea."

"Oh my, oh my," Sebastian said, scurrying about nervously.

In came the Sea King. Sebastian drew himself up stiffly, then bowed low. "Greetings, O grand and glorious and noble and gracious King! Your humble and lowly servant Sebastian is greatly honored by your visit!"

The mermaids rushed toward the bearded King with a chorus of "Hello, Father!"

"Greetings, my daughters," King Triton said, smiling. "Good afternoon, Sebastian. How are the rehearsals for the gala coming along?"

"The princesses are . . . fine, uh, superb, no, magnificent, Your Highness!" Sebastian stuttered. "They are achieving new heights of musical glory!"

The mermaids eyed each other and hid their grins. They knew well that Sebastian would never say anything to upset their father.

The King smiled. "Good, good," he said proudly.

Suddenly Andrina had an idea. "Father!" she cried out. "Sebastian has wonderful news!"

At once Alana knew what her sister was up to. "Oh, yes, Father," she said. "Listen to this. Sebastian has been invited to be a guest conductor at the Dixieland Waters Jazz Festival!"

King Triton was clearly pleased, and he beamed at Sebastian. "That is certainly excellent news! Sebastian, I am delighted to know that your fame has spread throughout the seas. You have my permission to attend."

"Thank you for your kind words," Sebastian replied. "But Your Majesty, I cannot attend."

King Triton's bushy white eyebrows went up. "And why is that?"

"Because I must stay here and work with your daughters," Sebastian said. "The gala is only three weeks from now, and we have a great deal to accomplish."

King Triton frowned. "You cannot decline this invitation, Sebastian."

"But Your Majesty," Sebastian protested, "my first responsibility is to the royal family."

"Your first responsibility is to the kingdom!" King Triton corrected. "If you refuse to go to the jazz festival, you could offend the merpeople of the Dixieland Waters."

"But Your Majesty . . . ," Sebastian began again.

"You will go!" King Triton stated decisively. "And I will not take no for an answer." He pointed his trident at the quivering little crab. "Sebastian, I command you to attend the jazz festival!"

Andrina winked at the others. They all knew that Sebastian would never refuse a command from the Sea King.

Sebastian bowed. "Yes, Your Majesty. I will go. But what will be done about the gala?"

"Maybe we could skip the gala this year," Andrina suggested hopefully.

Sebastian was shocked. "Skip the gala? Impossible! It is an annual event!"

King Triton cast a stern eye at Andrina. "Sebastian is correct, Andrina. The date has already been announced, and my guest, the Grand Mer-Rajah, has already accepted his invitation. My daughters, you are expected to perform, and that is what you will do," he said firmly.

"Who will direct the princesses, Your Majesty?" Sebastian asked.

King Triton thought for a moment. "As the

oldest, Aquata will supervise their rehearsals. She is a mature and responsible young woman, and I have no doubt that she will do a good job."

There was pride all over Aquata's face. "Thank you for your trust and faith in me, Father. I will do my best."

"Then it is all settled," King Triton said. "Sebastian, go and prepare for your journey."

Sebastian bowed and backed out of the hall. But as he crawled away, he stole a last glance at the mermaids.

"Good luck, Sebastian!" they called, waving with a little too much enthusiasm. "Have a wonderful time!"

"Now, my daughters, I have other duties to attend to," King Triton said. "You may continue with your rehearsal."

As soon as the King left, the mermaids began to dance with joy. "This is fantastic!" Alana squealed. "No scolding, no yelling, and no singing the same song over and over and over again!"

"Sebastian will be miles away!" Adella sang out. "We're on our own!"

Andrina was so gleeful, she did a backflip.

"And no more daily rehearsals!"

"Wait a minute, all of you," Aquata said. "You heard what Father said. I'm in charge now. I'll decide about the rehearsals."

The mermaids stopped and looked at her. Ariel sighed. "Aquata's right. With or without Sebastian, we still have to perform at the gala."

"That's true," Arista said.

"And I have to prove to Father that I can handle this, in a mature and responsible manner," Aquata said. She patted her brown hair, piled high on her head. She'd been wearing it that way so she'd look more grown up.

"But there's no law that says we have to put on a *musical* gala," Andrina noted slyly.

"Maybe this is our chance to try something new," Ariel piped in. "Like Attina's play!"

All the mermaids looked at Aquata anxiously. Aquata frowned. "I don't know. Father expects a concert, and—"

Alana interrupted. "He said he expects us to *perform*. He didn't say sing."

Arista looked uneasy. "But that's what he *meant*."

Andrina turned to Aquata. "You want to

27

impress Father with the way you handle the gala, don't you?"

"Of course," Aquata replied.

Andrina continued. "Then don't you think he'd be impressed if we did something different, something more original this time?"

"Maybe," Aquata said slowly. She thought for a moment. "I think we'd all better go to Attina's room," she said finally.

"My room?" Attina asked. "Why?"

Aquata smiled. "So you can read us your play!"

4

Back at the palace, the mermaids gathered in Attina's bedroom.

"This is exciting," Andrina said.

"Yes," Alana agreed. "It will be so much fun to put on a play instead of an ordinary concert."

"Don't get too excited," Aquata cautioned them. "We still haven't decided if we're putting on Attina's play."

"That's right," Arista piped in. "Besides, we don't know anything about the play. It might be terrible."

"Tell us about your play, Attina," Aquata said.

Attina blushed slightly. "Well, like I told you, it's about seven sisters. And that's the name of it—*Seven Sisters*."

"I like it," Andrina announced. "Let's do it."

"Hush," Aquata said. "Go on, Attina."

Attina continued with the story. "Their names are Zora, Zena, Zelda, Zally . . . " She hesitated. "I haven't named the rest of them yet. I couldn't think of any more names beginning with *Z*. Anyway, each one of the sisters is special in some way. One of them can dance."

All eyes turned to Aquata, who had studied ballet and was very good at it.

"Another one can sing," Attina said, and all eyes shifted to Ariel.

"One sister is a great athlete," Attina went on. Andrina grinned and took a dramatic bow.

"And another sister is very beautiful."

Adella preened. "Why, thank you, Attina."

"Wait a minute," Attina protested. "Adella, this play is fiction, not fact. It's not about a real family of sisters." She continued to describe the characters. "Another one of the sisters is a talented juggler, and another is a great artist."

Alana had been counting. "That's only six sisters. You said there were seven."

"The seventh is Zelda," Attina told her. "She doesn't think there's anything special about her."

"Well, I know which one *I* want to play," Adella stated.

"Gee, let me guess," Arista said, pretending to concentrate. "The beautiful one?"

"Does the athletic sister get to do a lot of backflips?" Andrina asked eagerly. "I can do a triple."

Ariel spoke up. "I don't think we should act the roles that we're most like. The audience might think the play is really about us."

"Don't start choosing your parts yet," Aquata told them. "I still haven't decided if we're doing this. I want to hear more about *Seven Sisters.* What happens, Attina?"

Attina told them the story. "Zelda is very lonely because each of her sisters is busy singing, or dancing, or doing whatever she does. They hardly ever even speak to each other. Zelda has to come up with a way to bring them all together. And she finally does."

"Father would like that kind of story," Andrina noted. "He's always talking about how important it is for us all to get along with each other."

"The play sounds nice," Ariel said.

"How does Zelda bring the sisters together?" Aquata asked.

"Well, she tells her sisters—" Attina didn't get to finish. She was interrupted by the King's sea horse messenger. "Your father wishes to see all of you," he said to the mermaids. "He is at the palace gate bidding farewell to the royal composer."

The sisters hurried out of the room and swam to the palace entrance. Sebastian, clutching a tiny suitcase, stood beside the King.

"Sebastian is about to leave for the jazz festival," their father announced. "He is traveling by flying fish, and his flight leaves in a few minutes. But he has something he would like to say to you first." He turned to Sebastian. "Have a pleasant journey. And bring credit to our kingdom!"

"I shall do everything within my power to honor you," Sebastian gushed, bowing low as King Triton left the palace.

Ariel couldn't tell if Sebastian was nervous, or sad, or excited—or maybe he had all of those feelings. When he spoke, his voice was shaky.

"My dear princesses, I feel that I am abandoning you! I hope you are not too distressed by my departure."

"Not a bit," Andrina said cheerfully.

"Of course, we'll miss you," Alana said quickly. "But we'll manage."

"You have a good time at the festival," Arista chimed in. "Don't think about us at all."

Sebastian raised a claw to brush away the trickle of a tear. "How can I not think about you? It pains me to think I will miss your performance." He turned to Aquata. "My dear, the gala is in your hands. I have the utmost faith in you. I know that you will direct your sisters well. I have no fear, no concern at all."

"Then why are you trembling?" Adella asked bluntly.

Sebastian fumbled with his words. "Well, I,

uh, er, I have a fear of flying."

Aquata placed a gentle hand on his claw. "Don't worry about us, Sebastian," she said softly. "I won't let you down."

"Good luck," the mermaids chorused, and they waved as he scurried away.

"Can we start practicing *Seven Sisters* now?" Attina asked.

Aquata sighed. "I'm sorry, Attina, but we can't perform *Seven Sisters* for the gala. I'm sure it's a fine play, and maybe we can put it on another time. But we owe it to Sebastian to present a concert, just as he planned it."

No one could miss the disappointment on Attina's face. Ariel felt terribly sorry for her. "Come on, Aquata," she pleaded. "Sebastian isn't even going to be here for the gala."

"That's right," Adella said. "And what he doesn't know won't hurt him."

"He'll find out when he returns," Alana pointed out. "And he'll be very upset."

"But it will be too late for him to do anything about it . . . but yell," Andrina argued.

"What about Father?" Alana asked. "He's expecting to hear a concert."

Arista shivered. "He's going to be awfully mad."

Attina brushed that comment away. "But when he sees how well we perform the play, he won't mind."

Aquata was annoyed. "Didn't any of you hear what I said? There's no point in arguing. I'm sorry, Attina, but we just can't do your play. We're doing the concert."

Andrina folded her arms across her chest. "Well, maybe *you're* doing a concert, Aquata. But we're doing *Seven Sisters*." She swam over to Attina.

"Don't speak for all of us, Andrina," Alana said. She moved to Aquata's side. "I'll sing with you, Aquata."

"Me, too," Arista said. "I don't want to risk having Father mad at me!"

"I vote for the play," Adella said, joining Attina and Andrina. Ariel hovered uncertainly between the divided sisters.

"What about you, Ariel?" Attina asked. "Will you be in my play?"

"I'd *like* to," Ariel said.

"But you have to be in the concert," Aquata insisted. "We need your voice!"

Ariel's eyes shifted from Attina to Aquata and back to Attina. What could she do? She didn't want to hurt either of them.

"Which is it?" Andrina demanded to know. "The concert or the play?"

Ariel sighed. She couldn't decide. Then she brightened. Maybe she wouldn't *have* to decide. She grinned at her sisters. "How about—both?"

The next morning, Attina led Ariel, Adella, and Andrina to a large empty cave not too far from the palace.

"I discovered this cave last week," Attina told them. "It's big enough for our rehearsals."

Adella wrinkled her nose as she gazed around the murky cave. "Why can't we practice in the concert hall?" she asked.

"We don't dare," Attina said. "Father might stop by to see how the rehearsals are coming along. We can't let him know about *Seven Sisters* until the night of the gala."

"It's going to be an awfully long gala," Andrina remarked. "Performing both a play *and* a concert."

"I don't care how long the gala lasts," Attina said. "I just want my play to be better than the concert. Ariel, how are you going to practice for both?"

"It's easy," Ariel said. "I just have to race from one rehearsal to the other. No problem."

"Well, I can think of a problem," Andrina said. "There are seven sisters in Attina's play. And there are only four of us."

"Couldn't you change the play?" Ariel suggested to Attina. "Call it *Four Sisters* instead of *Seven Sisters.*"

Attina shook her head. "We'll just double up on the roles."

Adella was confused. "Huh?"

"Each of you will play two parts," Attina said. "Of course, this means we'll have to work twice as hard."

The water rippled, and they turned to the cave entrance to see who was there. "Hello, Flounder," Ariel said.

"What's going on?" he asked. "What are you doing in here?"

"Can you keep a secret?" Ariel asked. Flounder nodded eagerly. "We're practicing a play for the gala," she told him. She explained how the sisters had split up.

"Can I watch you practice?" Flounder asked.

"No," Attina said without thinking. "No audience, no onlookers—" she clapped a hand over her mouth. "Oh dear, I sound just like Sebastian! I'm sorry, Flounder."

"We're just getting organized," Ariel explained to her friend. "Once we start real rehearsals, you can watch."

"I know something you can do," Adella said. "Go over to the concert hall and tell us how the rehearsals there are coming along."

Flounder agreed, and he left.

"Now," Attina said, "let's get to work. The play begins with all the sisters onstage. I guess I'll have to change that to just four of them."

"Shouldn't you tell us what parts we're playing?" Adella asked. "I want the biggest part."

"Zelda has the most lines," Attina said.

"Okay, Adella, you can be Zelda, and also Zora, the painter."

"But I want to be the beautiful sister," Adella complained.

Attina glared at her. "I'm in charge here, and you'll play the parts I tell you to play. Ariel, you'll play Zoey, the athlete, and Zena, the dancer."

Ariel nodded, but inside she was groaning. Dancing wasn't one of her talents.

Attina pointed to Andrina. "You're going to be Zally, the juggler, and Zorinda, the beauty. And I'll be the singer." She frowned. "I still haven't come up with a name for her."

"How about Zuzu?" Ariel suggested.

"Good," Attina said. "Now, Adella, Zelda has the first few lines. As you say them, each character comes onstage. Say, 'My sisters are all wonderful people. Each of them is very special in her own way.'"

"Okay," Adella said.

There was a moment of silence. "Say the lines," Attina said to Adella.

"Uh, I forgot them already," Adella confessed. "Could you tell me them again?"

Attina's tail twitched impatiently, but she

repeated the lines for Adella.

"That's too much to remember," Adella complained. "Can't I just say, 'I've got great sisters'?"

"No, you can't," Attina replied. "You have to say the lines properly. And you'll have to memorize them, of course."

"Memorize them!" Adella cried in dismay. "But Sebastian always lets us have our music in front of us when we sing in the gala."

Attina was getting annoyed. "This isn't a concert, it's a play. Now say your lines!"

Adella opened her mouth. Then she shut it. "I forgot them again."

It went on this way for more than an hour. Attina would give Adella her lines, Adella would argue about them, and by the time Attina ordered her to say them, Adella would have forgotten them.

"Adella, just sit and study your lines for a while," Attina finally said. "We'll work on the next scene. Zena, the dancer, is on the stage. Zoey, the athlete, is practicing somersaults and bumps into her. Zena gets angry."

"I think this is going to be a very difficult scene," Ariel said.

"Why?" Attina asked, growing more and more irritated from all the complaining.

"Because I'm Zena *and* Zoey," Ariel replied. "How can I bump into myself?"

Attina groaned. "Okay, I'll switch Zoey and . . . Zorinda. Zorinda walks across the stage and bumps into Zena."

Adella looked up in interest. "Zorinda is the beautiful one, isn't she?"

"Yes," Attina replied. "Andrina, you're Zorinda. You and Ariel, come here and I'll teach you your lines."

Adella was trying to study the script, but she couldn't help watching the others. Even though Attina had said that the play wasn't about the princesses, Adella was certain that Zorinda was based on *her.* And she couldn't wait to see what Attina had written.

"I think we're ready to practice the scene," Attina said. "Ariel, Zena has the first line."

Ariel pretended to be dancing, and she recited her lines. "I love to dance. Dancing means more to me than anything else."

Andrina approached, swishing her tail back and forth. "I have so much to do today," she said in a high squeaky voice. "I must try on five shades of lipstick. I want to try ten new hairstyles. I need to find at least fifty mirrors to admire myself in."

With a stern swoosh of her tail, Adella rose and swam over to her sisters, pointing an accusing finger at Andrina. "I don't act like that!" she angrily exclaimed.

"Zorinda isn't *you*," Attina said. "She's a made-up character."

"But everyone is going to think she's me," Adella wailed. "Everyone is going to think I'm so . . . so . . . so vain!"

Andrina giggled. "Well, you *do* spend a lot of time in front of mirrors," she pointed out.

"See!" Adella screeched.

Just then Flounder swam into the cave.

"Did you see the concert rehearsal?" Attina asked him eagerly.

"I saw it," Flounder said. "But I couldn't really hear it from the back of the hall. I think they need more singers."

"Well, they've got another one now," Adella declared. She gave Andrina one last, furious look and swam out of the cave.

6

As soon as the play rehearsal was over, Ariel sped through the water toward the concert hall. When she arrived, she found Aquata, Arista, and Alana waiting for her. Adella was there, too.

None of them looked very happy. "You're late," Aquata snapped at Ariel. "Ariel, you must be on time for these rehearsals. You have a lot of practicing to do."

"More than usual," Arista said. "You see, Sebastian wrote solos for you, Andrina, and

Attina, and since Andrina and Attina aren't singing, you're going to have to do their songs."

"I am?" Ariel asked faintly. "That's a lot of music to learn! I have to learn three parts now for *Seven Sisters*, too!" She couldn't resist shooting a glare in Adella's direction.

"Don't blame me!" Adella replied hotly. "I wanted to be in Attina's play. It was my chance to be a star! I'd sing one of the solos, but Aquata won't let me."

"That's because none of the songs are right for you," Aquata told her. She sighed. "How is *Seven Sisters* coming along, Ariel?"

Ariel knew Attina would be furious if she told the truth. "Fine," she lied. "The play is going very well. How was your rehearsal?"

"Just fine," Aquata said, although something about the tone of her voice told Ariel that she wasn't exactly telling the truth, either.

Aquata handed Ariel some sheet music. "Here's your first solo. You sing this verse, and we join in on the chorus."

The other mermaids gathered around Ariel. Aquata signaled to Octavio to begin the music, and she raised Sebastian's baton. Ariel opened her mouth and began to sing.

This time, however, a sweet melody didn't pour forth. Her voice was weak from hours of rehearsing the play, and she was so tired, she barely made it through the first verse.

The others joined in on the chorus. Ariel noticed that Aquata was frowning. Then Aquata rapped her baton and signaled for them to stop.

"Something's wrong," she said. "This song doesn't sound right at all."

Ariel recognized what the problem was. "It's the high notes. They're missing."

"Attina's the only one of us who can hit those notes," Arista pointed out.

"Well, let's go on to the next song," Aquata said.

But there were lots of high notes in all the songs. Nothing sounded right, and Aquata knew it never would. Sebastian had composed songs for seven sisters—not five.

"We'll just practice harder than usual," she said. "And we'll do the best we can." But Ariel had a sinking feeling that their best wasn't going to be good enough for the gala.

They sang for another hour. "We can take a

break for lunch now," Aquata announced.

But there would be no lunch for Ariel. She didn't have time to eat. She was already late for the next play rehearsal.

She left the concert hall and swam rapidly back toward the cave. "Ariel! Wait up!"

Looking over her shoulder, she saw Flounder swimming behind her. "I can't stop!" she called. "Catch up with me!"

Poor Flounder was out of breath by the time he reached her. "Are you having another rehearsal?"

"Yes," Ariel told him. "Maybe Attina will let you watch now." She certainly hoped so. Rehearsing for both a concert and a play wasn't going to leave her any time to spend with Flounder.

Attina and Andrina were waiting at the entrance of the cave. "You're late!" Attina told Ariel.

"Sorry," Ariel said. "But I have to do *your* solos in the concert, and Andrina's, too."

Andrina's mouth fell open. "Sebastian wrote a solo for me? Wow!" Her eyes were wistful.

"Don't even *think* about the concert,"

Attina instructed her. "We've got plenty to do here." She looked at the script in her hand and sighed. "I wrote a play for seven sisters, and now there are only three."

"You wrote this play yourself?" Flounder asked. He was impressed. "That's wonderful, Attina!"

His admiration cheered her a little. "Thanks, Flounder. You can stay and watch us practice. Maybe you can tell us how we're doing."

Flounder settled down to watch, and Attina gave instructions. "Andrina, now that Adella has quit the play, you're taking over the part of Zelda, so you've got the first lines."

Andrina began. "My sisters are all wonderful people. Each of them is special in her own way. Zena is a great dancer."

Ariel/Zena twirled around. "I love to dance," she said. "Dancing means more to me than anything else." As she spun, she tossed her arms around and banged one against the wall of the cave. "Ow!" Then her tail got caught in a mass of seaweed, and she had to wiggle her whole body to get free.

Andrina started giggling.

"What's so funny?" Attina asked sharply.

"Look at her!" Andrina laughed. "She doesn't look like a great dancer, does she?"

"Just keep going," Attina said.

"My sister Zuzu is a wonderful singer," Andrina said.

Attina struck a pose. "Singing is my life, and I have no time for anything else."

Andrina said her next line. "My sister Zoey is a fine athlete."

Ariel started turning somersaults.

"Wait a minute, Ariel," Flounder said. "I thought your name was Zena. I'm confused."

Attina was rubbing her forehead and staring at her script. "I don't blame you, Flounder. *I'm* getting confused, too." She looked up at Andrina and Ariel. Her eyes filled with tears. "This isn't going to work," she said. "The next scene has Zelda with Zorinda. And now Andrina's playing both of those parts!"

"What can we do?" Andrina asked.

The cave was quiet as the three mermaids considered the problem. They must have all had the same idea at the same time—because suddenly all eyes were on Flounder.

"Why are you looking at me like that?" Flounder asked, frightened.

Attina spoke sweetly. "Flounder, how would you like to be an actor?"

* * *

When the concert rehearsal was over, Adella swam away from the others. She was feeling down and wanted to be alone.

She wasn't surprised when she learned that there were no solos for her in the concert. Even though she didn't like to admit it, she knew she didn't have one of the prettiest voices.

But Attina's play had been her chance to be a star! Maybe she had stormed out too soon. She decided to swim over to the cave and see what was going on.

Adella could hear voices coming from the cave as she approached. She stayed by the opening and peered inside. Then she gasped.

Flounder was there, with a ribbon from Attina's hair tied around him. He looked completely miserable.

"Now, say your line," Attina told him.

Flounder squeaked the words. "I need to find at least fifty mirrors to admire myself in."

Adella backed away from the cave. Her face was burning. So now they had a *fish* playing her! She'd be the laughingstock of all the merpeople when they saw that!

She was so upset, she almost missed seeing the merman who was passing by. "Good afternoon, Princess Adella," he said.

Adella forced herself to smile. "Good afternoon." She noticed that the merman was quite handsome, so she dipped her head slightly and gave him a flirty sidelong look.

"Are you having a pleasant day?" he asked.

"My sisters and I are rehearsing for the gala," she replied.

"Oh, yes, I'm looking forward to that," he said. "Lots of luck," he added as he swam away.

Adella was grinning from ear to ear when suddenly an image flashed before her eyes—Flounder was playing her onstage at the gala. And there was the handsome merman in the audience. He was laughing.

Her smile faded.

* * *

Ariel had never been so tired in her life. She barely had enough energy to drag herself down to dinner. When she finally made it to the dining room, all her sisters were already there, and so was her father.

"Ariel, you're late," King Triton said sternly.

Ariel wondered how many times she'd be hearing that in the days to come. And how many times she'd be saying, "I'm sorry."

"We have a guest," her father said. He turned to the distinguished merman sitting by his side. "This is my youngest daughter, Ariel. Ariel, this is the Grand Mer-Rajah of the Indian Ocean."

"How do you do," Ariel said politely.

The Grand Mer-Rajah bowed his head. "I am delighted to meet you. King Triton, you have seven lovely daughters. What a fortunate man you are."

"Thank you," King Triton replied. "I am very proud of my princesses. As you know, they are busy preparing for the annual gala. We are looking forward to having you as our special guest this year," he added.

"Your annual gala is quite famous," the

Grand Mer-Rajah said. "I'm delighted that I will be able to attend."

"You will enjoy it very much," King Triton said. "Won't he, my daughters?"

The mermaids smiled and nodded. But as soon as King Triton drew the Grand Mer-Rajah into a conversation, their smiles disappeared. If the seven daughters of King Triton could read each other's mind, they would know they had something in common.

They were all *very* nervous.

One week later, Ariel was more than nervous—she was downright scared. Just as she suspected, all the practice in the world couldn't hide that there were voices missing in the songs Sebastian had written. And *Seven Sisters* as performed by three sisters and a fish wasn't any better.

At the concert hall, Aquata was making the mermaids sing "The Beauty of the Sea" for the tenth time that morning. None of them had to look at the sheet music anymore. They knew every word and note by heart.

"Oh, what a lovely sight," they sang. "Our ocean world by night." Suddenly they stopped.

"What's wrong?" Aquata asked. All the mermaids' eyes were directed behind Aquata, who whirled around and practically choked. King Triton and the Grand Mer-Rajah stood there.

"Good morning, Daughters," King Triton said. "We would like to sit in on your rehearsal today."

The Grand Mer-Rajah was counting. "I believe two of your daughters are missing, King Triton."

"Uh, they're, um, taking a break," Aquata stammered.

"We'll wait for them to return," King Triton said. "Is something wrong, Aquata? You appear rather pale."

"Oh, no, everything is fine," Aquata assured him. She cleared her throat. "But, you see, we, um . . . "

Ariel jumped in. "We want the gala to be a surprise, Father. We have something special planned. So we're not allowing any visitors."

King Triton gazed at her suspiciously.

"Visitors? I am not a visitor. I am your father!" Then he said to Aquata, "Just what kind of surprise are you planning?"

Adella came to the rescue, letting out a tinkling laugh. "Now Father, if we told you, it wouldn't be a surprise, would it?"

The mermaids waited with bated breath for their father's response. Finally, to their relief, he smiled. "I understand," he said, and turned to his guest. "Come, I will take you on a tour of our kingdom." When he reached the exit, he ushered the Grand Mer-Rajah out the door. Then the King turned and spoke to the sisters again.

"Daughters, I want you to know that I am very proud of you. I know that you are working hard to make the gala a success. Sebastian will be proud of you, too." He chuckled. "You know, he did not think you would be able to handle this on your own. But I assured him that with Aquata in charge, you would be fine. And I am confident that you will prove me right." And with that, he departed.

For a moment the mermaids were silent. Aquata tapped her baton and raised it, and they all started singing again.

Ariel winced. It was a beautiful song, but it sounded flat. Aquata burst into tears.

The other mermaids rushed to her side. It wasn't like Aquata to cry. She always tried to act so dignified. But here she was, sobbing her heart out.

"Sebastian worked so hard on these songs," she wept. "They're glorious songs. But we're ruining them! The songs are going to sound terrible! We've betrayed him, and he's going to be devastated!"

Ariel tried to comfort her. "It's not your fault, Aquata."

"It *is* my fault," Aquata insisted. "Father put me in charge. He has faith in me—he thinks I'm mature and responsible, remember? What is he going to think when the concert is a disaster? When he sees that I've failed, he'll never trust me again!"

Because of the way Aquata was feeling, practice ended early. For once, Ariel could make it to the *Seven Sisters* rehearsal on time.

The atmosphere in the cave wasn't much happier than the mood in the concert hall. Poor Attina was still trying to arrange her play so that two characters played by the same actor wouldn't have to be onstage at the same time.

Andrina was playing Zelda. "I must think of a way to bring my sisters together," she recited. "Perhaps Zoey could teach Zora to turn somersaults. Zoey! Zoey!"

Ariel somersaulted onto the scene. "Here I am, Zelda. What do you want?"

Then Andrina turned to the other direction and called, "Zora! Zora!"

Ariel stopped short. "I'm Zora now, too. How can I teach myself to turn somersaults?"

"I guess I'll have to be Zora," Attina said.

"But you're Zuzu," Ariel pointed out. "And Zuzu has the next scene with Zora."

Attina frowned. "I forgot about that. Maybe Flounder can be Zora as well as Zorinda."

From a corner of the cave, Flounder moaned in despair.

"All right," Attina said. "We'll come back to this scene later. Let's move on to the next scene. Read your line, Ariel."

Ariel/Zoey turned to Andrina/Zally.

"Zally," she asked, "would you like me to teach you how to turn somersaults?"

"No," Andrina/Zally said. "I'd rather juggle." She scooped up a bunch of seashells. Then she froze.

"What's the matter?" Attina asked.

"I just remembered," Andrina groaned. "I don't know how to juggle."

"Alana does," Ariel noted.

"Alana is not in the play," Attina said sharply. "Maybe you can learn how to juggle before the gala."

"But that's just a week away," Andrina declared. "It's not easy to learn how to juggle."

"You'll manage," Attina snapped.

Ariel could see that Attina was getting more and more tense. "Andrina," she said hurriedly, "let's skip this part and move on."

"Okay," Andrina said. "We'll come back to this scene, too. In the next scene, I have the first line." She cleared her throat. "Zorinda! Zorinda!" she called.

Flounder swam toward her. He was so nervous, his voice squeaked. "Here I am. What do you want?"

"Would you like Zoey to teach you how to do somersaults?" Andrina asked.

"I'm too busy," Flounder said. "I'm brushing my hair."

Andrina cracked up. "Flounder, you're a fish! You don't have any hair!"

At that, Attina burst into tears. "You're right!" she cried. "He doesn't have any hair. The audience will laugh. Oh, this is terrible. How can we present this in front of Father? And the Grand Mer-Rajah? Not to mention all the merpeople who come to the gala?"

"If only we could get the others back," Andrina said sadly.

"Yeah," Flounder agreed. "Then I could be in the audience, where I belong!"

"*Seven Sisters* is a good play," Ariel said. "But we need seven sisters to be in it."

"Aquata and the others will never give up the concert," Attina said, sniffling. "Do you think the play is good, Flounder?"

"Oh, yes," Flounder said. "I like it, so far. I hope it has a happy ending."

"So do I," Andrina agreed. "We could all use some cheering up. How does *Seven Sisters* end, Attina?"

Attina wiped away a tear. "Well, Zelda has problems trying to make her sisters become closer. Finally, she gets an idea. She decides to put on a show and have all her sisters do what they do best. She finds out that she has a talent, too—bringing people together. The sisters have so much fun together that they finally realize how much they care about each other."

"That sounds nice," Flounder said happily.

On the other hand, Ariel had a jumble of thoughts running through her head. Finally, one clear idea emerged. "That's it! I've got it!"

"What?" Andrina asked.

"Come on!" Ariel yelled. "Follow me!"

She dashed out of the cave. Bewildered, Attina, Andrina, and Flounder followed.

When Attina saw that Ariel was leading them to the concert hall, she stopped. "Oh, Ariel," she moaned. "You want us to join them and do the concert. Well, I'm not giving up on *Seven Sisters*."

"You don't have to!" Ariel declared.

"What do you mean?" Attina asked.

Ariel's eyes were shining. "We're going to turn *Seven Sisters* into a musical!"

Inside the concert hall, Aquata was alone, studying Sebastian's music. When she saw Andrina and Attina, her face darkened. "What do *you* want?"

"Listen," Attina pleaded. "Ariel has a plan."

"A plan?" Aquata asked suspiciously.

"Aquata," Ariel said quickly, "I've been thinking. This is all so silly how we've been taking sides and fighting with each other over the gala. I think I've found a way we can

64

perform in the gala together and please everybody!" Ariel looked hopefully at her sister.

"How?" asked Aquata.

"Look," Ariel explained. "Sebastian's songs can fit right into *Seven Sisters*. See this one—'Have Fun with Me'—it would be perfect for Zelda to sing when she's trying to get her sisters to play with her. And 'Jumping for Joy' is just right for Zoey, the athletic mermaid."

Aquata looked over her shoulder at the sheet music. "That's the song Sebastian wrote for Andrina."

"Then Andrina will play Zoey," Ariel said. "Whatever we decide," she added, "*Seven Sisters* and Sebastian's music match up perfectly."

Attina was nodding. "You know," she said, "I think it would be best if each of us played the role we're most like. Aquata could be Zena, the dancer. Alana can be the juggler, and Adella can be the beauty, Zorinda."

"Only if you change some of my lines," Adella said. "I'm not going to help you be mean to me. Maybe I am too vain, but maybe

it's because I don't have as much talent as the rest of you. All I have is my looks. Is it so terrible if I try to make the most of them?"

"I'm sorry if I hurt your feelings," Attina said. "But you'll still have to ham it up a little."

"That's okay," Adella said. "I guess I won't mind that if I'm doing it myself. One problem, though . . . Who's going to play Zelda? That's the biggest part."

"Attina should play her," Ariel said excitedly. "After all, she wrote the play."

"No," Attina said, smiling. "Zelda is the sister who brings everyone together. That's what you're doing right now, Ariel. It's your part. What do you think, Aquata? Can we do this?"

They watched anxiously as Aquata considered the idea. And they all breathed a sigh of relief when she smiled.

"I think it's a brilliant idea!" Aquata declared. "In fact, it's perfect! We'll be doing something different and original, and we'll also be giving everyone what they want and expect."

"Best of all," Attina said softly, "is that

we'll be doing something *together*."

Flounder was looking very relieved, too. "And *I* won't have to act! But do you have enough time to prepare this?"

"We'll *make* time," Aquata stated firmly. "Let's get everyone together. We'll have to practice every single minute until the night of the gala. We're going to give this kingdom a show like they've never seen before!"

For the next five days, the mermaids spent every free minute they had rehearsing for the gala. Even at lunch- and dinnertime, they raced over to the concert hall, having already asked Cook to send the meals to them there.

As for *Seven Sisters*, the show was shaping up beautifully. The mermaids were pleased with the progress and grew more and more excited as the days passed. But nobody was happier than Flounder. As he watched them practice day after day, he smiled to himself, relieved that he didn't have to act after all. With that dumb ribbon tied around my head, he thought, I would have been the laughingstock of the sea!

Finally, the big night arrived. Minutes before their opening number, the mermaids scurried about backstage at the concert hall.

Aquata was chattering a lot more than usual. "It's strange," she said. "We've been working day and night for the past week. We ought to be terribly tired. But I'm not tired at all! I guess I'm just too excited."

"And maybe nervous?" Ariel suggested.

Aquata drew herself up and tried to look dignified. "Nervous? Not a bit."

Ariel grinned. "Then why are your scales quivering?"

"We're *all* quivering," Alana stated. "I just hope the audience thinks it's part of the show!"

"Now, now," Attina said. "We've worked hard, we know our songs and our parts, and we're going to be terrific. I can't think of one reason to be nervous."

"*I* can," Arista argued. "And his name is Father."

The sisters eyed each other uneasily. "Well, it's too late to worry about that now," Aquata declared. They could hear Octavio tuning his instruments. "It's almost showtime!"

The sisters gathered together and waited in the wings for their cue from Octavio. They all held hands, nervously giggling and whispering among themselves.

"Shhh . . . ," Aquata said. "It's time!"

The opening song began, and the mermaids sailed onto the stage. Ariel/Zelda swam around each sister, singing the first song.

It's fun to play,
On a beautiful day,
Under the sea.
Come along, join the song,
Have fun with me.

When she finished singing, she spoke. "My sisters are all wonderful people. Each of them is special in her own way."

"My name is Zena," Aquata said. "I like to dance."

"My name is Zally," Alana said. "I juggle seashells." One by one the sisters introduced themselves. Then Ariel spoke again.

"I am Zelda," she told the audience. "I don't do anything special." She hung her head and swam over to Attina. "Zuzu," she asked, "will you play with me?"

Attina pretended to ignore her and began her song.

Singing makes me happy,
Singing makes me glad,
I sing to lift my spirits,
Whenever I feel sad.

When Ariel/Zelda asked Zena the same question, she was ignored again. Aquata, as Zena, then sang about her talent.

Dancing's what I love to do.
I dance my cares away.
When I dance, I'm never blue.
I could dance all day.

It was amazing how each song that Sebastian had written suited the parts the mermaids were playing perfectly! When they finished, Ariel sang her song about being alone.

I know that I don't look like you,
But I will tell you something true,
I hope and pray, to find a way,
That we can still be friends.

It was a sad, sweet song. As she sang, Ariel

saw quite a few tears being shed in the audience.

Each of the other mermaids performed—beautifully—and then came the finale. Sebastian's most beautiful song—his pièce de résistance—had been saved for last. One by one the mermaids approached the edge of the stage and formed a line. They held each other's hands, and when they sang, a glorious sound rose high up into the stands of the concert hall. Ariel secretly wished Sebastian could have been there to hear their grand finale. She knew he would have been pleased.

It doesn't matter what you do,
Or if you're red, or green, or blue,
If you live in the sea, you belong.
Big fish, small fish, fat or thin,
Swimmers or crawlers, in a shell,
 with a fin,
If you live in the sea, you belong.
Dolphins, starfish, great big whales,
Even if you don't have scales,
If you live in the sea, you belong.

When the sisters finished, the audience cheered and applauded loudly.

"Encore! Encore! Bravo!"

Smiling proudly, Aquata motioned to her sisters to sing the finale again. This time the audience was so moved, they joined hands, claws, fins, whatever they had, and sang along.

And then it was over. The sisters threw their arms around each other, hugging, laughing, and crying, all at the same time.

"Daughters!" King Triton strode onto the stage. "You have done a superb job!"

The mermaids were so relieved. "Thank you, Father," they cried.

The Grand Mer-Rajah stood beside Triton. "That was brilliant!" he exclaimed. "When I return to my sea, I shall tell everyone about the multitalented daughters of King Triton."

"I am very proud of you all," King Triton declared.

"Father," Aquata said, "do you think Sebastian will be upset when he finds out that we changed the program?"

"I don't know," King Triton replied. "Why don't you ask him yourself?" He moved aside. There, directly behind him, was Sebastian!

He wore an enormous grin on his face, and he could barely contain his excitement. "That was magnificent!" he exclaimed. "Outstanding! Fantastic! Delightful! Never did I think of combining my songs with a story. It was a wonderful idea! My dear princesses, I am so proud of you all."

"Hurry back to the palace, Daughters," King Triton ordered. "I have invited Sebastian to join us in celebrating the triumph of the gala!" With the Grand Mer-Rajah, he got into his chariot and rode off.

"Sebastian, how was the jazz festival?" Ariel asked.

"Ah, it was wonderful!" Sebastian beamed. "You should have seen me—I had them all on the edge of their seats! I was the toast of the Dixieland Waters! All that applause, and . . . " He stopped and cleared his throat. "Yes, but . . . ahem, er . . . I was worried so about you all. Terribly worried. Was it difficult for you, preparing the gala on your own?"

The mermaids exchanged sly looks. "Not at all," Aquata said quickly.

"We had no problems," Alana assured him.

"Everything went beautifully," Attina added.

All that fibbing made them uneasy, but no one wanted to distress Sebastian. To their surprise, he didn't look at all pleased with their responses. He was looking down at the ground, shaking his head.

"Then you didn't need me at all," he said sadly. "You managed just fine on your own."

Ariel rushed forward and hugged him. "Oh, Sebastian, that's not true!"

Attina bit her lip. "It wasn't easy at all!" she confessed. "Why, I was in tears!"

"Me, too," Aquata said. "We were barely speaking to each other!"

"The gala was almost a total disaster," Andrina reported.

Sebastian's eyes widened. "Really?"

The mermaids nodded, and Sebastian beamed.

"Now *that's* music to my ears," he said happily.

The mermaids burst out laughing. Then, linking arms, they swam off to join the party. They had a lot to celebrate—the gala, Sebastian's return . . . and each other.